Be Awesome & Keep Shining!

Christy Ziglar

Shine Bright Kids™
Choose Right. Shine Bright.

Must-Have Marvin!

Written by
Christy Ziglar

Illustrated by
Luanne Marten

ideals children's books.
Nashville, Tennessee

ISBN-13: 978-0-8249-5657-8

Published by Ideals Children's Books
An imprint of Ideals Publications
A Guideposts Company
Nashville, Tennessee
www.idealsbooks.com

⭐ **Shine Bright Kids™**

Color separations by Precision Color Graphics,
Franklin, Wisconsin
Printed and bound in China

Library of Congress CIP data on file

Designed by Georgina Chidlow-Rucker

Leo_Dec13_1

DEAR GROWNUPS,

We all know that it's fun to get new things from time to time; and all of us want to provide for our children. But how do we teach them that relationships give our lives meaning and purpose, not things? Do our kids see us investing in others, or are we simply focused on "providing" for our own family's needs and entertainment? How much time and energy do we spend accumulating more stuff? Do our children know the difference between wants and needs?

Look for ways to encourage your kids when they are investing in others. Instead of always rewarding with a new toy, consider using a reward chart. We use "Star Charts" with "Star Points" that can be redeemed not just for stuff, but experiences and adventures, a special project, time alone with Mom or Dad, or simply quality time together as a family.

Visit **www.ShineBrightKids.com** for games, apps, tools, and parenting resources to help your family choose right and shine bright!

Christy Ziglar

In honor and loving memory
of Zig Ziglar, 1926-2012.

—CZ

For my family.

—LM

You can have lots of stuff,
but it will never be enough.
Instead, make lots of friends,
and you'll be happy in the end.

STAR SEARCH!

Find the star that follows Marvin!
Can you tell whether it is excited
or sad? When Marvin makes wise,
thoughtful decisions, the star looks
happy and bright. When Marvin
makes choices that might not be
the best, the star looks dim and
deflated. On each page, notice the
star's mood and try to guess why
it might feel that way.

"You can have everything in
life you want, if you will just
help enough other people get
what they want."

—ZIG ZIGLAR

Marvin jumped out of bed and put on his brand-new dinosaur T-shirt. The instant he'd seen it at the store, he'd yelled,

"I HAVE to have it!"

He couldn't wait to show the kids at school.

Marvin loved new things!
He liked learning new things and
making new things and playing
new games.

But most of all, he liked getting
the latest, greatest, coolest
new stuff.

Marvin was excited as he walked to class—until he spotted Oscar wearing the same shirt! And Oscar had matching **glow-in-the-dark** shoes!

Marvin had just one thought:

"I HAVE to have them!"

Later, his classmates were planting their corner of the school vegetable patch.

They called, "Marvin, come help!"

But Marvin sat on the bench all alone, dreaming about those amazing shoes.

On Wednesday, they were learning about different instruments in music class.

Marvin heard one blast of the trumpet and declared,

"I HAVE to have one!"

While practicing for the Parents'
Night concert, Marvin was so busy
pretending to announce the arrival of the
king and queen that he bumped into Wanda.

This started a chain reaction that did not end well.

At recess, Marvin saw something he really wanted! It was a SUPER GALACTIC ROBOT—the coolest, most awesome toy ever!

Marvin shouted,

"I HAVE to have one!"

It was all Marvin could think about that afternoon. He was so busy dreaming about the robot he wanted that he didn't help Willy with their science experiment.

It was a two-person job.

The next day, Marvin was still talking about the robot at soccer practice.

"I HAVE to have one!"

he said again and again.

Coach suggested he take a time-out, since his head wasn't really in the game.

The team was collecting box tops for a special trip. Willow asked, "Marvin, will you help me count the tops?"

"Sorry," Marvin replied, as he rushed off the field.

"There is something I HAVE to do!"

As he passed Mrs. Bailey's house, she called out, "Marvin, dear, would you help me get this recycling together?"

"Sorry, Mrs. B.," Marvin called back. "There is something I HAVE to do."

At home, his brother Sammy wanted to practice throwing.

"Sorry," yelled Marvin. "There is something I HAVE to do!"

Marvin found the catalog with the SUPER GALACTIC ROBOT on the cover. He counted all the money in his piggy bank, including his secret reserves.

He had just enough.

Marvin put on his best smile and proudly held up the catalog.

"What's that?" his mother asked.

"It's a SUPER GALACTIC ROBOT!" Marvin exclaimed. "It's the coolest, most awesome toy ever, and

I HAVE to have one! I just HAVE to!"

"Now, Marvin," asked his father, "are you sure? You will be spending all your money."

"Yes, Dad!" said Marvin, "I HAVE to have it!"

"All right," his father said. "We can go after dinner, when your homework is done."

Marvin was so excited! He searched the shelves until he found it—the exact robot he'd been dreaming of!

He had it out of the box before they even left the store. He turned it on and heard the robot say, "HELLO. I AM A ROBOT. I AM AT YOUR SERVICE. LET'S PLAY."

That night, Marvin imagined all the fun he was going to have with his very own

SUPER GALACTIC ROBOT!

After school on Friday, Marvin wanted to show the robot's spinning tricks to Sammy.

"Sorry," said Sammy. "Oliver is helping me with my throwing."

Marvin went to see if Willow wanted to play. She would be impressed with the laser eyes.

"Sorry, Marvin," Willow said. "I have to finish counting the box tops for the team."

He went to Oscar's house next. But Oscar had gone to the movies with Wanda.

Marvin wished his robot would say
something to cheer him up.

All it said was, "HELLO. I AM A ROBOT.
I AM AT YOUR SERVICE. LET'S PLAY."

Marvin missed his friends.
He started home alone.

As he passed Mrs. Bailey's house, she asked, "Marvin, what's wrong?"

Marvin replied, "I wanted this robot more than anything, but now that I have it, I don't feel happy. I just feel lonely."

"Marvin," Mrs. Bailey explained, "things won't make you happy, only people can. If you'll spend more time helping your friends and less time thinking about new stuff, you'll be a lot happier.

"By the way, doesn't your team have a soccer game tomorrow?"

Oh no! Marvin had forgotten about the game and the team project! He had been so busy thinking about his new toy that he hadn't collected a single box top.

Marvin had let his friends down.

Mrs. Bailey had an idea. "Marvin," she said, "Do you have time to help me with the recycling now?"

"I guess so," Marvin said. He got to work.

As he folded the empty boxes and stacked them, he noticed that some of the boxes had the tops that the soccer team needed for their trip.

He counted ten!

"Mrs. B.," Marvin yelled, "can I keep these box tops?"

"Of course!" she said, with a knowing smile.

"Thanks so much, Mrs. B!"
he shouted as he ran home.

When he woke up Saturday morning, Marvin reached for his SUPER GALACTIC ROBOT—but then he stopped.

He could hear Mrs. Bailey's advice in his head.

He flashed the laser eyes on and off and then placed the robot on the shelf.

He picked up his baseball glove and headed downstairs.

Marvin threw the ball with Sammy until Sammy was ready for his afternoon game. Marvin had forgotten how much fun playing catch was.

As he dressed for the soccer game, Marvin thought about bringing his robot along.

Instead, he grabbed the orange soccer ball that was Oscar's favorite for warming up.

At the field, Willow and Coach were sharing the results of the team project. "Thanks for all your hard work," said Willow, "but I'm afraid that we still need ten box tops."

Everyone was disappointed.

"Wait!" Marvin yelled as he ran up to the group. "Mrs. B. had ten more box tops!"

"Now we can all go on our trip!" said Willow.

"Hurray!" everyone cheered.

It was the best day ever!

As they left the field, Willow asked, "Marvin, what new stuff do you HAVE to have for our trip?"

Marvin grinned. "The only things I really HAVE to have are my FRIENDS!"